This book belongs to

HARRISSH

Written by Nick Page.
Illustrated by Clare Fennell.

Oh, no, Mr. Snowman!

Clare Fennell • Nick Page

make
believe
ideas

"Come on! Let's build a snowman!"

Katy said to me.

So we did.

We built a snowman, Katy and me,

and we called him "Mr. Snowman".

We played with Mr. Snowman all afternoon, Katy and me,
and when it got cold, Mum called us in for tea.

* FROSTY *

- jelly
- yule log
- ice cream
- pudding

We ate our tea, Katy and me.

But something was wrong.

The fish fingers were still frozen,
the beans were crunchy with frost
and our hot chocolate was **really cold.**

Then we saw him . . .

Can you see him?

* FROSTY *

- jelly
- yule log
- ice cream
- pudding

Oh, no, Mr. Snowman! You CAN'T come in here!

We played with Mr. Snowman the next day, Katy and me,
and when it got late, Mum called us in for story time.

But something was wrong.

My book had frozen shut,
the sofa was covered in snow
and the room was **really,**
really cold.

Then we saw him . . .
Can you see him?

Oh, no, Mr. Snowman! You CAN'T come in here!

Cats are allowed indoors, snowmen aren't.

We played with Mr. Snowman the next day, Katy and me,
and when we got tired, Mum called us in to have our bath.
But something was wrong.

Our towels were as hard as wood,
there were icebergs in the bath
and the water was **really, really,**

really cold.

Then we saw him . . .
Can you see him?

Oh, no, Mr. Snowman! You CAN'T come in here!

And STAY OUT!

We played with Mr. Snowman the next day, Katy and me,
and when it got dark, Mum called us in and took us to bed.
But something was wrong.

My pillow was like a lump of ice,
Katie's teddy bear was frozen solid
and we were **really, really,
really cold**.

Then we saw him . . .
Can you see him?

Oh, no, Mr. Snowman! You CAN'T come in here!

Say "No" to snowmen!

The next day… it was Christmas Eve!

All of our family came to stay.

But something was wrong.

The ice cream was runny,

the jelly wasn't set

and everything was **really, really,**

really hot!

The fridge had broken!

Then there was a
knock at the door.

Knock!
Knock!

Who could it be?

Oh, yes, Mr. Snowman. You **CAN** come in here!

Mr. Snowman iced all the ice creams
and set all the jelly.
Mr. Snowman made
everything snowy!

Happy Christmas, Mr. Snowman!
Happy Christmas, Katie! Happy Christmas, Me!

Everyone was **really happy** that Mr. Snowman had come indoors.

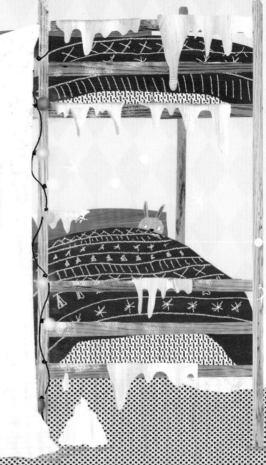

Ha, ha!

You can't catch me!

To Katie and Me

Well . . . almost everyone.